Mama and The Hanalei Sea Turtle

By Dylan Hazen

Illustrated By: Rebekah Anderson

Special thanks to those who helped fund this project on Kickstarter even though we did not reach our goal.

Russ Ronchi and Wendi Cohen, you guys were our top supporters. Thank You!

On the island
of Kauai,
in the town of
Hanalei...
Can be found the
famous pier,
where the children
like to play.

A pretty town with
rainbows and showers
And mountains said
to have magical powers

NENE
xing

To get to Hanalei,
you must take a one-way road
under which a river flows

A family of three
from California,
were happy
to have found
this amazing place
to hang around.

Somewhere over t

Year after year they came
to surf and play.
Their favorite place?
Hanalei Bay.

And in the winter,
the waves are as tall as a tree

While in the summer they are as small as a bee

But no matter how
big or how small
the wave

Off the pier
you jump,

to show that
you are brave!

Then one day, while kids were leaping into the sea, surfing by came that family of three

Suddenly the Mama cried out "Sea Turtle, Sea Turtle! Over there!"

The dad and the boy looked all about and yelled "where? where?!"

They searched and searched...
but no turtle could be found...
Mama said "I'm sure it's here!
Look around!"

The boy said
"Mama, you're
crazy!

Turtles
don't come
to the Bay,
they're too lazy!

This isn't
Turtle Cove
or a turtle station!

This all might be
in your
imagination!"

The boys continued
to surf, while
Mama continued
to look.
They caught a wave
and decided
they should
make this
into a book!

A book about a turtle that didn't exist.
Except to the Mama , boy did she persist!

Then as loud as can be Mama did yell
"TURTLE HEAD! Right there in the swell!"

And surfing right by,
who did appear?
A Hawaiian Green
Sea Turtle,
This time it was clear!

As often goes...

The boys were wrong,
and Mama was right!

The Hawaiian Green
Sea Turtle,
or Honu, right
there in plain sight!

On the island of Kauai, in the town of Hanalei...
Can be found a Happy Honu surfing in da Bay!

The End.

Moral of the story...
Listen to your mama!

About The Author

Dylan Hazen surfing in Kauai

This is a true story. Dylan wrote this book (with our help) while on vacation in Kauai. For two years, "mama" swore she saw a sea turtle in Hanalei while surfing, but Dylan and Dad never saw it. Dylan decided to write the book while sitting in the Pacific on a Stand-Up Paddle board.

Love Mom and Dad

Dylan Hazen is 7 years old and resides in Huntington Beach, CA This is his first book.